j398.8   Grant, Vernon,
GRA   1902-
2004
/C   Vernon Grant's Mother
LC 2015   Goose.

$9.95

DATE			

Mother Goose

Illustrations by Vernon Grant

HARRY N. ABRAMS, INC., PUBLISHERS

ACKNOWLEDGMENTS

It is my pleasure to acknowledge and thank those who helped the Museum of York County in working with Harry N. Abrams, Inc., and Kellogg Company to create this tribute to the art of Vernon Grant: our marketing representative Shirley Henschel of Alaska Momma, Inc.; Museum Trustees J. Spratt White and Allan Miller, and former Trustee Linda Williams; Diane Dickey, Alinda Arnett, and C. A. Kate McGinn at Kellogg Company; and Robert Morton at Harry N. Abrams, Inc. Thanks also to the members of the Museum's Board of Trustees and Vernon Grant Committee, as well as the Vernon Grant Estate, for their leadership and vision in preserving the legacy of Vernon Grant. A special thanks to Mary Lynn Norton, the Museum's Curator of Art, whose devotion to her work is an inspiration to us all.

Van Shields
Director, Museum of York County

CREDITS AND PERMISSIONS

The following illustrations are used with permission. Courtesy of Kellogg Archives: © 1933, 1998 Kellogg Company, pp. 18 and 30; © 1938, 1998 Kellogg Company, p. 16; © 1939, 1998 Kellogg Company, pp. 11, 21, 23, 26, and 27. The characters *Snap!® Crackle!® Pop!®* are trademarks of Kellogg Company. Kellogg's® Rice Krispies® are trademarks of Kellogg Company. All other illustrations are from the Vernon Grant Estate Collection. © 1998 Museum of York County. All rights reserved.

Editor: Robert Morton
Designer: Darilyn Lowe Carnes

Library of Congress Cataloging-in-Publication Data
Grant, Vernon, date.
   [Mother Goose]
   Vernon Grant's Mother Goose / illustrations by Vernon Grant.
        p.   cm.
   Summary: Illustrations by the creator of Snap!, Crackle!, and Pop!
accompany a collection of familiar nursery rhymes, including "Little
Jack Horner," "Old King Cole," "Humpty Dumpty," and "Simple Simon."
   ISBN 0–8109–4128–7 (hardcover)
   1. Nursery rhymes.   2. Children's poetry.   [1. Nursery rhymes.]
I. Title.
PZ8.3.G7424Ve   1998
398.8—dc21   97–31157

Harry N. Abrams, Inc.
100 Fifth Avenue
New York, N.Y. 10011
www.abramsbooks.com

THE RHYMES

Twinkle, Twinkle Little Star

TWINKLE, TWINKLE, LITTLE STAR,
How I wonder what you are.
Up above the world so high,
Like a diamond in the sky.

When the blazing sun is gone,
When he nothing shines upon,
Then you show your little light,
Twinkle, twinkle all the night.

JACK BE NIMBLE,
Jack be quick,
Jack jump over the candlestick.

Tom, Tom the Piper's Son

Tom, Tom, the piper's son,
Stole a pig and away he run.
The pig was eat,
And Tom was beat,
And Tom ran crying down the street.

DEEDLE, DEEDLE, DUMPLING, MY SON JOHN,
Went to bed with his stockings on.
One shoe off, and one shoe on,
Deedle, deedle, dumpling, my son John.

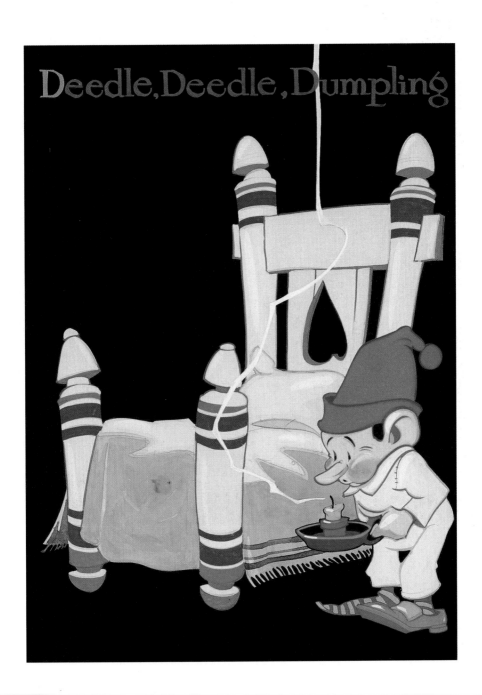

LITTLE JACK HORNER

Sat in the corner
Eating a Christmas pie.
He put in his thumb,
and pulled out a plum,
And said, "What a good boy am I!"

Jack Spratt

Could eat no fat.
His wife could eat no lean.
And so, betwixt them both, you see
They licked the platter clean.

Sing a song of sixpence,
A pocket full of rye.
Four-and-twenty blackbirds,
Baked in a pie.

When the pie was opened
The birds began to sing.
Wasn't that a dainty dish
To set before the king?

The king was in the counting house
Counting out his money.
The queen was in the parlor
eating bread and honey.

The maid was in the garden,
Hanging out the clothes,
When down came a blackbird
And snapped off her nose.

OLD KING COLE WAS A MERRY OLD SOUL,
   And a merry old soul was he.
      He called for his pipe, and he called for his bowl,
      And he called for his fiddlers three.

         Every fiddler had a fine fiddle,
         And a very fine fiddle had he.
           "Twee, Tweedle-dee, tweedle-dee," went the fiddlers.
          Oh, there are none so rare as can compare
           With King Cole and his fiddlers three.

There was an old woman of Harro

ho visited in a wheelbarrow

THERE WAS AN OLD WOMAN OF HARROW,
Who visited in a wheelbarrow.
And her servant before
Knocked loud at each door
To announce the old woman of Harrow.

THERE WAS AN OLD WOMAN WHO LIVED IN A SHOE.
She had so many children she didn't know what to do.
She gave them some broth without any bread,
She whipped them all soundly and sent them to bed.

A WISE OLD OWL LIVED IN AN OAK

A WISE OLD OWL LIVED IN AN OAK.
The more he heard, the less he spoke.
The less he spoke, the more he heard.
Why aren't we all like that wise old bird?

HUMPTY DUMPTY

HUMPTY DUMPTY SAT ON A WALL,
Humpty Dumpty had a great fall.
All the king's horses and all the king's men
Couldn't put H together again.

u
m
p
t
y

PETER, PETER, PUMPKIN-EATER,
Had a wife and couldn't keep her.
He put her in a pumpkin shell,
And there he kept her very well.

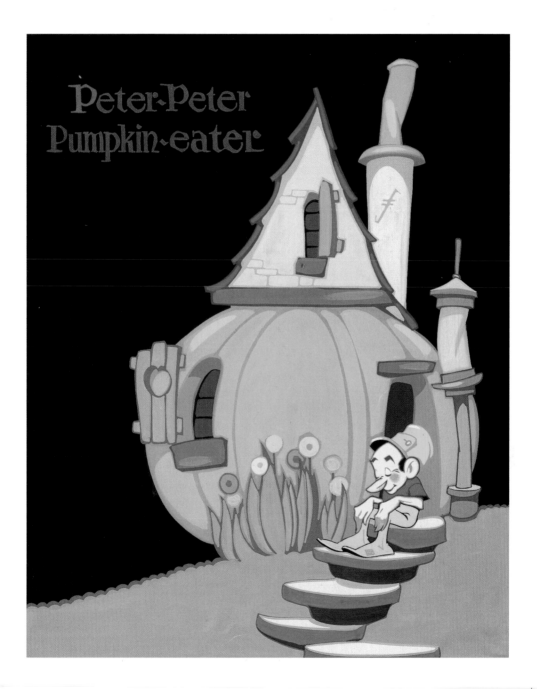

Jerry Hall, he was so small,
A rat could eat him hat and all.

JERRY HALL,
He was so small,
A rat could eat him,
Hat and all.

and he found a crooked six-pence

THERE WAS A CROOKED MAN,
And he walked a crooked mile,
And he found a crooked sixpence
Against a crooked stile.
He bought a crooked cat,
Which caught a crooked mouse,
And they all lived together
In a little crooked house.

Rain, rain, go away
Come again another day,
Little Johnny wants to play.

"RUB~A~DUB~DUB"

Rub-a-dub-dub,
    Three men in a tub,
    And who do you
think they be?
    The butcher, the baker,
        the candlestick maker.
    They all jumped
out of a rotten potato,
    Turn 'em out,
        knaves all three!

Nose, nose, jolly red nose,
And what gave thee that jolly red nose?
Nutmeg and ginger, cinnamon and cloves,
That's what gave me this jolly red nose.

LADYBUG, LADYBUG,
Fly away home!
Your house is on fire, your children all gone,
All but one, and her name is Ann,
She crept under the pudding pan.

Simple Simon

SIMPLE SIMON MET A PIEMAN
Going to the fair.
Says Simple Simon to the pieman,
"Let me taste your ware."

Says the pieman to Simple Simon,
"Show me first your penny!"
Says Simple Simon to the pieman,
"Indeed, I have not any."

Simple Simon went a-fishing
For to catch a whale.
But all the water he had got
Was in his mother's pail.

Simple Simon went to look
If plums grew on a thistle.
He pricked his finger very much,
Which made poor Simon whistle.

He went to catch a dicky bird,
And thought he could not fail,
Because he had a little salt
To put upon its tail.

He went for water in a sieve,
But soon it all ran through.
And now poor Simple Simon
Bids you all adieu.

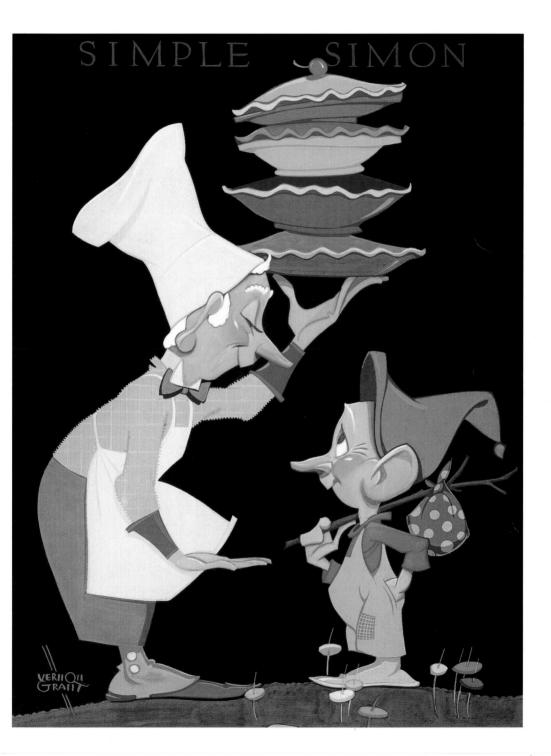

FRIDAY NIGHT'S DREAM
On the Saturday told,
Is sure to come true,
Be it never so old.

"How Many Miles to Babylon?"

How many miles is it to Babylon?
Three score miles and ten.
Can I get there by candlelight?
Ay, and back again.
If your heels are nimble and light,
You'll get there by candlelight.

Little Tee Wee

He went to sea
In an open boat.
And while afloat,
the little boat bended,
And my story's ended.

VERNON GRANT, ARTIST AND ILLUSTRATOR

Renowned as one of the giants of American illustration, Vernon Grant created thousands of drawings and paintings for advertising products and magazines over the course of more than sixty years.

Born in Nebraska in 1902, Grant was the son of a blacksmith with a pioneering spirit who moved his family to the rugged plains of South Dakota in 1908. Life in South Dakota was difficult; the Grants lived hundreds of miles from the nearest major city. Everything they needed they made themselves, beginning with the sod house in which Vernon and his brother grew up. There were few luxuries, and Vernon soon learned to make his own toys from the clay by the riverbanks. The little figures he modeled were forerunners of the colorful, winsome gnomes that would later launch his career as an illustrator.

Vernon's parents encouraged his early artistic efforts, but the person who made the greatest impact on his life was his cousin, Nellie Grant, a schoolteacher. Adventurous and high-spirited, she had been educated at the Art Institute of Chicago, and she studied art in France and Italy before making her way west. She gave Vernon a solid grounding in art and design and supported his belief that he could become a famous artist.

When Grant was a teenager, the family moved to California, and he entered the University of Southern California at Los Angeles in 1921. Two years later, at the age of twenty-one, he enrolled in the Art Institute of Chicago, where facing competition for the first time was a shock to him. In high school and college he had been considered a fine artist, but here he was only another student. He soon realized that it was his fantasy illustrations—mainly gnomes and imaginary insects—that gained attention and made him stand out. His gift was a flair for make-believe, and using this gift to his fullest he graduated with honors.

Following graduation in Chicago, Grant moved back to the West Coast and spent the next five years in Los Angeles teaching art. Many of those who studied with him later went to work for Walt Disney as animation artists. Grant landed several advertising accounts in Los Angeles, but he knew that he would have to go to New York City to succeed as a commercial illustrator.

In 1932 he left Los Angeles, as the story goes, with only $11 in his pockets. But he had a great determination and a willingness to work hard. He was down to his last quarter when he had his first stroke of luck—a commission to design playing cards using the gnome characters he had developed since his student days. Soon, other commissions, including some for magazine covers, began to flow in; he worked for *Judge* (which gave Ted Geisel—better known as Dr. Seuss—and James Thurber their first breaks), *Ladies Home Journal, Collier's,* and many other major publications.

Grant's illustrations are varied and many, but his best known creations are the elfin *Snap!, Crackle!, and Pop!* characters for Kellogg Company. Each weekday during the 1930s, a familiar radio sign-on ("Good afternoon, girls and boys—Kellogg's Singing Lady is on the air") was heard in millions of American homes. Long before Saturday morning cartoons, the Singing Lady, alias Irene Wicker, delighted youngsters by reading nursery rhymes and singing songs on her NBC radio network show. It was from listening to this popular children's program that Vernon Grant first visualized the creation of the trio that changed the future of a struggling breakfast cereal and launched the struggling artist on the road to international fame.

Within a short time, Grant's influence on Kellogg Company's advertising campaigns extended beyond the creation of *Snap!, Crackle!, and Pop!* When a clever marketing technique was developed to include the Singing Lady's stories on the backs of cereal boxes, Grant became the illustrator for the whimsical tales and popular nursery rhymes that appeared there. The stories and their illustrations grew so popular that Kellogg Company began including box-top coupons that families could mail in to receive elaborate full-color story and song booklets, large prints, decals, children's notepads, ink blotters, and much more—all illustrated by Vernon Grant. Such merchandising efforts firmly established Rice Krispies as the premier children's cereal and helped "Kellogg's Singing Lady" radio program to become America's most popular children's show for an entire generation.

Within a few years, Grant's popularity as a children's artist was so firmly established that Kellogg sent him on a world tour to promote its cereals. Upon his return in 1935, Grant made guest appearances on the Singing Lady's show, where she told stories about the artist's humble childhood on the bleak South Dakota prairie. By 1938, *Life* magazine was referring to Grant as "America's favorite children's artist." Other memorable commercial creations of Grant's include "Salty the Sailor" for the Sterling Salt Company, "Aunt Rennie" for Junket Rennet Puddings, and a sixty-year-long tradition of annual depictions of Santa Claus.

The full extent of Vernon Grant's nursery rhyme work during the 1930s and 1940s is unknown. At least ten booklets, more than twenty-five individual prints, hundreds of different cereal box illustrations, and dozens of toys and premiums illustrated by Grant and published during the period have been documented. Nursery rhyme premium offers also were commercially contracted with Junket Rennet Puddings and Wright's Silver Cream, a household polish.

Grant spent much of World War II with the USO (United Service Organizations) performing humorous illustrated sketch talks to entertain wounded troops. After the war Madison Avenue no longer had the same appeal for him, and in 1947, Grant moved with his wife and two small children to Rock Hill, South Carolina. There, he became a successful and respected farmer, although he continued to produce commercial art and spent months each year in New York City. Even after his trips north ended, Grant went on creating illustrations well into the 1980s. He lived in Rock Hill until his death in 1990.

Vernon Grant's style of illustration was distinctly his own. An honored member of the Society of Illustrators, Grant contended that fantasy was not a suitable study in art school. He once wrote that art, "must be developed by the individual through his own personal imaginative powers and through life experiences." Grant's imaginative powers and inventive childhood artmaking experiments were catalysts for the inspiration that made him a standout in the world of illustration.

His whimsical gnomes and humorous caricatures appeared in print from the 1920s through the 1970s on everything from magazine covers to product packaging, billboards, greeting cards, children's books and store displays. His commercial clients included General Electric Company, Hershey Food Corporation, and Eveready Flashlight Batteries.

Political cartoonist Art Wood, in his book *Great Cartoonists and Their Art*, stated: "While Grant's work was imitated, it was never emulated. His style was distinctive and influenced such diverse artisans as Walt Disney, Russell Patterson, Don Flowers, and Walt Scott. He had a gift for color, and his vivid poster-like paintings decorated children's rooms around the world. Grant had a genius for crisp, imaginative characterizations and rarely since Arthur Rackham, the British illustrator, has anyone captured the elusive quality of youth as well as this talented artist did."

Today, much of Vernon Grant's original art is housed at the Kellogg Company archives in Battle Creek, Michigan, and at the Museum of York County in Rock Hill, South Carolina. The Museum of York County's Vernon Grant Gallery opened in 1979 as a permanent home for hundreds of his paintings, illustrations for children's books, magazine covers, and advertisements. The Vernon Grant Collection is a wonderful reflection not only of the artist's amazing talent but also of the times in which he lived.

Mary Lynn Norton
Curator of Art
Museum of York County